A Wolf in the Woods

First published in 2009
by Wayland

This paperback edition published in 2010 by Wayland

Text copyright © Penny Dolan 2009
Illustration copyright © Kirsten Richards 2009

Wayland
338 Euston Road
London NW1 3BH

Wayland Australia
Level 17/207 Kent Street
Sydney, NSW 2000

Series Editor: Louise John
Editor: Katie Powell
Cover design: Paul Cherrill
Design: D.R.ink
Consultant: Shirley Bickler

A CIP catalogue record for this book is available from the British Library.

ISBN 9780750257428 (hbk)
ISBN 9780750260381 (pbk)

Printed in China

Wayland is a division of Hachette Children's Books,
an Hachette UK Company

www.hachette.co.uk

A Wolf in the Woods

Written by Penny Dolan
Illustrated by Kirsten Richards

WAYLAND

The family were wandering through the forest, searching for somewhere to set up camp.

"Let's stop here," said Pa. "This was a safe spot last year."

"No place is safe from wild animals until there's a strong fire burning," warned Grandpa. "We'll need to collect some wood."

Ma made a hollow in the ground. She filled it with a twist of soft dry grass. Then she took out her fire flints and struck them together until she made a spark.

"Quick, come and help, children," Ma called.

Luli and Ma puffed away until a tiny flame grew, and the grass began to smoke.

Luli's brother, Erg, took the very last pine cones from the sack he was holding, and placed them on the small fire. They started to burn.

"Shall we go and look for more pine cones?" asked Luli.

"That's a good idea, but hurry back," called Ma.

The children ran into the woods and filled their sacks with cones. Soon they forgot to hurry and began to play amongst the trees.

"Hoo! Hoo! I can call like an owl,"
said Erg.

"Look! I'm a deer," said Luli, and
she ran through the woods with
her arms raised above her head
like antlers.

Then Erg took a deep breath and howled a strange long howl. The noise pierced the air and echoed through the trees.

"I can make that sound too," said Luli. "Aaaarooooooo! Aaaaarooo!"

At that moment, the sun dipped behind a cloud, and the woods grew dark. Then the children heard another noise.

"Did you hear that?" whispered Luli urgently. "It sounded like growling!"

"It came from over there," gasped Erg. "Something's watching us. Quick, let's hurry back to camp!"

The children raced home as fast as they could. Over their shoulders, they saw a shadow moving through the trees.

"I'm sure it's following us,"
Erg said, panting.

Suddenly, Erg tripped over a fallen tree branch that was stuck in the ground.

"Ahh!" he cried, as he fell with a thud.

Luli ran back to help him. "Come on!" she whispered frantically, pulling on his arm. "We have to hurry!"

"But I can't get up!" Erg groaned, as he clutched his leg. A large cut was visible on his knee. It was bleeding.

"You have to," said Luli, as she helped Erg gently to his feet. "Come on!"

Luli began to lead Erg back to camp.
"It's not far now," she said.

Erg's knee was so painful that the children had to travel slowly, but they dared not stop. The shadow seemed to be getting closer and closer.

At last, they reached the edge of the camp and saw the fire burning.

Pa came running towards them.
"What happened?" he asked, as
he scooped Erg into his arms and
carried him to the fire.

"Pa, look!" called Luli. "Something's
after us!"

A thin and bedraggled wolf stood watching from the trees. When the wolf saw the flames blazing up from the fire, she turned back.

"That wolf's been hurt, too," said Pa. "She's limping."

"You're safe now," Ma said, hugging Luli. "Don't worry. The fire will stop her coming closer."

That night, as the family sat around the fire, Erg and Luli told them about the wolf in the woods.

"You were lucky the wolf had been injured," said Ma. "If she had been able to run, you would have been in trouble."

"Still, it's too dangerous to have an adult wolf living so close to this camp," said Pa. "Tomorrow we must go and hunt it."

The next day, Pa, Grandpa and the uncles gathered their spears and headed into the woods.

"I'll help you look for paw prints on the ground," said Luli.

Luli and the men followed the wolf's tracks until they reached some rocks.

"That's where her den must be," said Pa.

However, as the group approached the den, they saw the thin wolf lying dead on the ground. She had old spear wounds in her leg and side.

"Oh, that's sad," cried Luli. "Poor wolf!"

"Think how sad we'd have been if that wolf had caught you or Erg," said Pa. "Besides, this wolf will help us survive, Luli. Her thick fur will keep us warm this winter."

The men picked up the dead wolf,
ready to take her back to camp.
At that moment, Luli heard whimpering
coming from within the den.

"What's that?" asked Luli.

"I think I know," answered Pa, peering inside the mouth of the den. Then, reaching in his hand, he pulled out a tiny wolf cub that was crying for its mother.

"Oh, Pa, can I keep it?" asked Luli, as she took the cub gently in her arms. It snuggled down contentedly.

"Well," said Pa thoughtfully, "I've heard that it's possible to tame wolf cubs, but it will be hard work," he warned. "You must remember to feed him every single day."

"I won't forget," said Luli, firmly. "Please, Pa!"

Just then, the little wolf club wriggled from Luli's arms. It struggled over to Pa's feet, and lay on its back on the ground.

Pa chuckled, and, bending down, tickled the small creature's tummy. "See, he likes you!" cried Luli.

"Well, this little one isn't dangerous yet," laughed Pa. "Come on, Luli, let's take him home!"

START READING is a series of highly enjoyable books for beginner readers. **The books have been carefully graded to match the Book Bands widely used in schools.** This enables readers to be sure they choose books that match their own reading ability.

Look out for the Band colour on the book in our Start Reading logo.

The Bands are:

Pink Band 1A & 1B

Red Band 2

Yellow Band 3

Blue Band 4

Green Band 5

Orange Band 6

Turquoise Band 7

Purple Band 8

Gold Band 9

START READING books can be read independently or shared with an adult. They promote the enjoyment of reading through satisfying stories supported by fun illustrations.

Penny Dolan enjoys writing stories on her computer at home, and sharing stories with children in schools and libraries. Penny also likes reading, painting and playing djembe drums. She has two grown-up children and one bad cat.

Kirsten Richards lives in a small house near Oxford with her two cats, three plants and more spiders than she'd like to contemplate. When freed from her duties of cat food opener and chin scratcher, she draws and paints to her heart's content.